MESSAGE
IN A BOTTLE

Published in the United States by Random House Children's Books, a division of Penguin Random House LLC, 1745 Broadway, New York, NY 10019, and in Canada by Penguin Random House Limited, Toronto. Random House and the colophon are registered trademarks of Penguin Random House LLC.

ISBN 978-0-399-54962-5 (trade) — ISBN 978-0-399-54963-2 (lib. bdg.)
ISBN 978-0-399-54964-9 (ebook)

randomhousekids.com

Printed in the United States of America
10 9 8 7 6 5 4 3 2 1

MESSAGE IN A BOTTLE

By Victoria Saxon

Illustrated by Artful Doodlers

Random House 🏠 New York

PROLOGUE

One morning, on what seemed like an ordinary beach day, Barbie, Skipper, Stacie, Chelsea, and their loyal puppies were faced with a major mystery— Raquelle's missing jewelry! It was a tough case, but by working together and using their sleuthing skills, the sisters were able to track down the missing jewels— with the help of their puppies, of course.

After the case was closed, the sisters were determined to leave no mystery unsolved—no matter how tricky. The Sisters Mystery Club was formed, and no secret was safe from the super sleuthing sisters!

CHAPTER 1

Barbie took a deep breath of fresh air as she looked out at the ocean near her house. It was a beautiful day. The sun had warmed the sand, and cool breezes ruffled the puppies' fur as they ran toward the shore with Barbie's sisters.

"Barbie, let's build a sand castle!" Chelsea called to her oldest sister.

"And let's play beach soccer!" added

Stacie as she kicked a soccer ball to Barbie.

Skipper switched on her tablet. "Or play video games," she said.

Barbie smiled. There was definitely lots to do, but it might be difficult to get her sisters to agree on one plan.

"Sounds good," Barbie said, "but let's go visit Teresa at the lifeguard station first." Barbie and her friend both worked at the beach as lifeguards.

Woof! Barbie's puppy, Taffy, barked. *"Ooh, those waves look big,"* the puppy said to her siblings. *"Stay near the lifeguard!"*

"*There's good digging sand near the lifeguard shack,*" Rookie added.

As the puppies scrambled through the sand, Barbie laughed. Sometimes it seemed as if the puppies were talking to each other, but of course, they couldn't talk.

Barbie and her sisters headed up the beach, with the puppies at their feet.

"*Maybe Teresa has some of those peanut butter treats!*" DJ barked.

"*Oh, yum! Race you!*" Rookie shouted.

When Barbie stopped and put her

hand up to shield her eyes from the sun, she spotted her friend Teresa on lifeguard duty. Teresa was scanning the beach with a pair of binoculars. There were some surfers riding the waves. A couple was jogging with their dog. Some teenagers were setting up a game of volleyball. Teresa was keeping a safe watch over all of them.

Barbie, her sisters, and the puppies continued along the shore until they reached the lifeguard station.

"What's she holding?" asked Honey.

"I don't know," Taffy answered, "but it doesn't look like peanut butter treats."

Teresa turned to greet her friends. She was holding four sandy bottles in her arms.

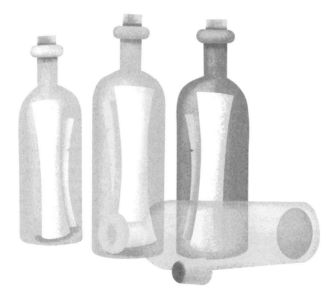

"Barbie, I'm so glad you're here," Teresa said. "I found these bottles—and each one has a piece of paper inside. I think they might be secret messages!"

CHAPTER 2

Teresa told Barbie and her sisters that when she started lifeguard duty that morning, she had noticed something shining under an old, overturned boat. When she looked closely, she had found four bottles underneath.

"I opened one of them and saw this," Teresa said.

Barbie unfolded the piece of paper that

Teresa handed her. It didn't look like a message at all.

"It's just a red circle and an *M*," said Chelsea.

The paper was torn along two sides.

"I know," said Teresa. "I don't get it."

Barbie looked at Teresa. "Did you say there were more messages in the other bottles?" she asked.

"Yes," Teresa replied as she handed the bottles to Chelsea, Barbie, and Stacie. "I really want to solve the mystery, but I'm on lifeguard duty all day. Can you help me out, Barbie?"

"Of course we can," Barbie told her.

"Sounds like a job for the Sisters Mystery Club," said Chelsea.

"We'll get to the bottom of this," Skipper said.

"And let you know what we find," added Barbie.

"See you later!" Chelsea waved to Teresa.

"Thanks," Teresa said as she walked back to her station. "Good luck!"

"I'm going over to the boat to look for

more clues," Skipper said as she pulled out her smartphone. "And I'll take some photos, which will help us keep track of the evidence."

"I'm going with her!" DJ said as he tumbled through the sand.

"Me too!" said Rookie. *"You might need a good digger!"*

Chelsea giggled as she watched the puppies stumble across the sand. "I'm following Skipper and those puppies," she said as she ran after them.

Barbie and Stacie trailed them with

the other puppies.

The overturned boat was small and white with oarlocks on either side. It had red trim. There were footprints all around it.

"Those look like adult-size footprints," Chelsea said.

"Boots," Stacie commented.

The puppies sniffed near the boat and found some paw prints, too.

"Those look like grown-up dog prints," Honey said to the other puppies.

"Maybe that dog knows something about

the bottles. Let's track her!" Rookie said.

"My sniffer's ready," added DJ.

Barbie looked around the beach. "Let's see what the other messages are," she said. As the wind gusted around them, the sisters huddled close to one another with the puppies. They pulled a note from each of the three bottles. One had a small sketch of a star and the letter *N* written on it. The next one had a picture of a white horse with a spot on its forehead and the letter *E*. The third one had a picture of a shack and the letter *S*.

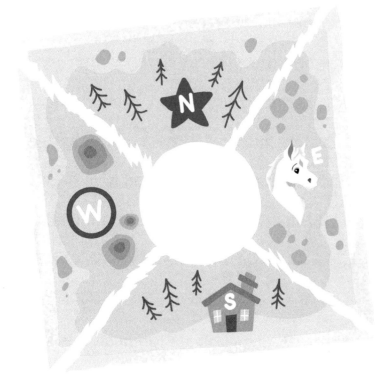

"I think I know what the *M* means on the first piece of paper," Skipper said excitedly. "Barbie, can I see that paper for a second?"

"Sure!" Barbie handed her the first clue. Skipper turned it upside down.

"That *M* is a *W*," she declared. "*N* for north, *S* for south, *E* for east, and *W* for west. These pieces of paper are sections of a map!"

"Hey!" Chelsea exclaimed. "This is like that treasure map in Willows. I know how to put this together. Piece of cake!"

Chelsea set to work.

When she was done, Barbie said, "There's a circle missing in the middle of the map."

"Yeah, but what does it mean?" asked Stacie.

Chelsea grabbed Barbie's hand. "Maybe it's a hidden pirate treasure!"

"*Woof!*" Honey barked.

Barbie, Chelsea, Skipper, and Stacie turned to look at the puppies. There was something left in one of the bottles. Rookie was rolling the bottle in the sand.

Something shiny glittered in the sunlight. It made a clinking noise. . . .

CHAPTER 3

"Stand back!" DJ warned.

"No worries here," Taffy said. *"I'll stand way back."*

Barbie picked up the bottle and tipped it into her hand. A coin fell out.

"That's a silver coin, isn't it?" Skipper asked.

Barbie looked closely at the coin. "Yes," she said. "And there's a message:

'Find the silver treasure before it's too late!'"

Skipper took the coin and turned it over. "Look! Someone put a black X in the middle," she said. "I wonder if this—"

"—goes right in the middle of the map!" Chelsea finished.

Barbie put the coin in the middle of the map. "Bingo!"

"I'm going to explore under the boat," said Rookie.

Stacie looked at her puppy digging.

"Did you find something, Rookie?" she asked.

Rookie jumped back up the sand bank. Stepping behind him, Skipper and Stacie peered under the boat.

Rookie crawled in the sand and barked again.

"Rookie has something!" Stacie shouted.

Sure enough, the puppy pulled something black and lumpy from under the boat.

"It's a boot!" Chelsea said.

"Two boots," added Stacie.

"I'll take a picture of them," Skipper said as she leaned down and focused her phone on the old boots. "They must belong to somebody."

Then Skipper did a search on her phone. "The map shows some horse ranches inland, to the east."

"Maybe we can find the horse that's

on the map," Stacie said as she looked up the beach.

"This mystery is getting more mysterious by the minute," said Barbie. "Now that we have all the pieces of the map, let's see if we can find the silver treasure!"

CHAPTER 4

The sisters and the puppies walked along the beach until they reached a rocky point that jutted out into the water.

"The only way around that is"—Skipper turned so her back was to the water— "to the east. Let's go inland."

The sisters called to the puppies and went up and around the point. Together, they climbed over some boulders and

walked along a grassy shoreline before heading back to the beach.

Then Taffy barked. The puppy was standing next to Barbie, and both their eyes were set on a barn to the north.

"Look! There's a barn with a star painted on the roof!" Barbie called to her sisters.

"That matches the star to the north on our map!" Stacie said.

Skipper pulled out the map and looked at it again. "According to this, there's a little shack to the south."

"I can see it!" Stacie added, pointing to a small lifeguard station just south of them on the beach.

"Look out on the water!" Chelsea said. "There's a big red buoy."

"That must be the red circle to the west on the map!" Skipper exclaimed.

Barbie looked at the map and then looked inland. She saw a small ranch with a house, a stable, a brown fence, and a lot of sea grass.

"I don't see any signs of a horse to the east," she said.

"Wait!" Chelsea exclaimed.

She pointed to something in the middle of the grassy field. There was a sign in front of the stable. It had a picture of a

horse—with a spot on its forehead!

"That's our horse clue!" exclaimed Stacie. "It's to the east."

Skipper turned the map. "We've found all the coordinates on the map," she said.

The puppies began barking. To the left of the house, there was a banner flapping in the breeze.

"Look!" Stacie called to her sisters. "That banner—it has a skull and crossbones."

"A pirate flag!" Chelsea exclaimed.

"It also looks like a big X," Skipper added.

CHAPTER 5

"**L**ooks like we found the X on the map," Barbie said. "Now what?"

The puppies continued barking.

"We can climb up there and dig for treasure," Chelsea suggested.

"We can't go up there," said Barbie. "It's someone's home."

"Hey, I know that smell," Honey said to her siblings.

"*Last one there's a rotten egg*," barked DJ.

All four puppies scrambled up a grassy bank toward the ranch.

The sisters chased them, but the puppies kept running. Soon they started climbing some wooden steps that rose from the beach to a house with a blue door. The pirate banner waved overhead.

"Rookie!" Stacie called out. "No trespassing!" She stood on the sand at the bottom of the steps. Her sisters gathered near and called to the puppies.

"Where are they going in such a hurry?" asked Skipper.

Chelsea grabbed Barbie's hand. "What if they're chasing a pirate ghost?"

Just then, a large brown-and-black collie appeared at the top of the steps and barked at the puppies. She seemed friendly.

"So that's what the puppies were interested in—they wanted to meet that big dog," Skipper said.

A woman in a floppy sun hat walked up behind the collie. She was carrying a bag of dog treats. She gave one to her dog, then laughed and tossed some treats to the puppies.

"Score!" shouted DJ as he gobbled up a treat. *"They're peanut butter!"*

"That lady's nice!" added Honey as she ate one, too.

The woman called down to Barbie and her sisters. "Do you want to come up here? I think your puppies want to meet my dog, Nika."

Barbie looked at Taffy, Rookie, Honey, and DJ and smiled. "Our puppies never

pass up snacks—or a new friend."

"That lady doesn't look like a scary pirate," Chelsea added.

Together, the sisters climbed the steps. The woman introduced herself. Her name was Catherine. She was a biologist and owned the ranch.

"Do you know about any silver treasure around here?" Chelsea asked. "We've been looking for a really long time."

"Tell me more," Catherine said. There was a twinkle in her eye as she added, "Did you by any chance find a map?"

"We did!" Stacie answered. "In four bottles."

"And a coin," added Skipper.

"With a black X," Chelsea explained.

Catherine stroked Nika's fur. "I put those messages in the bottles. It was a treasure hunt I set up for my niece and nephew. They're visiting from out of town. I thought it would be fun, so Nika and I put all the clues under that old rowboat. My niece and nephew love to sit on that boat at lunchtime to look for dolphins."

"Aha! It was Nika who made those pawprints around the rowboat," DJ barked.

Chelsea frowned. "Did we ruin your treasure hunt?"

"Not at all. I can give them another map." Catherine smiled. "You've just added to the fun. I'm thrilled that you solved the clues and found your way here."

"So . . . is there a treasure?" asked Stacie.

Catherine stood up and gestured toward the sandy beach below. "Your treasure will be right here, but it's not a pirate chest filled with silver."

"What is it, then?" Chelsea asked.

Catherine smiled. "If you come back here tonight after sunset, you'll see. . . ."

CHAPTER 6

"**I** can't wait to find the treasure," Stacie said.

"I can't wait to stay up late!" Chelsea exclaimed. "Mysteries use up a lot of energy. Good thing I took a nap."

Barbie and her sisters had called Teresa and told her all about the treasure map. They also told her to join them near Catherine's house to see the treasure.

"I knew it was a mystery," said Teresa. "Thanks for solving the puzzle. I'll meet you there."

When they reached the cove, the evening air was cool, and the sunset cast a beautiful golden light over the beach. Catherine greeted them. Her niece and nephew ran over to them excitedly.

"I gave them a copy of the map down by the beach," Catherine explained as she introduced everyone. "They followed the clues to this spot, too."

Catherine had put several beach chairs,

some blankets, and a picnic supper on her front lawn. She also had some binoculars and more dog treats.

"I told you I liked this lady!" Honey yipped.

Everyone relaxed and had fun eating and comparing notes on how they'd found the treasure spot.

"Now let's go find that treasure," Catherine said. "Look down at the beach, watch the tide roll in, and wait."

Barbie picked up a pair of binoculars.

The sisters sat away from the ledge

overlooking the beach. It grew darker as they watched the waves wash ashore for high tide. They saw clouds cover the moon and move away.

"Look closely at the sand," Catherine advised.

Suddenly, the puppies started barking. They jumped at the gate at the top of the wooden steps.

"This is weird," Stacie said, "but I think the sand is moving!"

"Yikes!" Chelsea said.

Teresa jumped to her feet. "Of course,"

she said excitedly. "I should have known!"

Barbie focused her binoculars and smiled in disbelief. "Is that . . . ?"

"The grunion are running," Catherine replied.

"The who are what?" asked Skipper.

They all looked down at the moonlit shoreline. It was high tide, and it seemed as if thousands of small silver fish were dancing on the sand.

"The grunion are fish. They come onto the beach at high tide," Catherine explained. "They lay their eggs and return to the sea. Now if you'll excuse me, I have to go down there to collect data about the grunion." She slipped an old pair of boots onto her feet.

"The boots! Those are the ones I took a picture of this morning," Skipper said, pulling out her phone to show everyone. "So you have special boots for this work?"

"Yes!" Catherine replied. "My niece and nephew might have understood that clue better than you girls. I always wear them when I go down to the water's edge."

The sisters and the puppies watched Catherine make her way down to the shore.

"Mystery solved," Stacie said. "Who would have thought the hidden treasure would be so beautiful?"

"I would!" Rookie barked.

Teresa, Barbie, and her sisters laughed. It was a beautiful night and a beautiful treasure. It was also a night on which the super sleuthing sisters would sleep well, having solved

yet another mystery . . . along with their

adorable puppies, of course!